W9-BER-426

8 3 9 16 9
2 4 5 3 18
4 6 17 7 8
1 3 14 9 20
15 4 2 5 6
7 9 1 10 2

Hello Kitty®

Hello Numbers!

Count 1 to 20 with Your Favorite Friend!

illustrated by Higashi Glaser

HARRY N. ABRAMS, INC., PUBLISHERS

hello one!

Hello Kitty is having a surprise party for someone very special.

Count her guests and the goodies as they arrive!

1

One hostess.

hello two!

2

Two cupcakes Kitty has baked.

hello three!

3

Three friends together!

hello four!

4

Four ice cream cones sparkle with sprinkles.

hello five!

5

Five friends together!

hello six!

6

Six candy apples are a yummy, gooey treat.

hello seven!

Seven friends together!

hello eight!

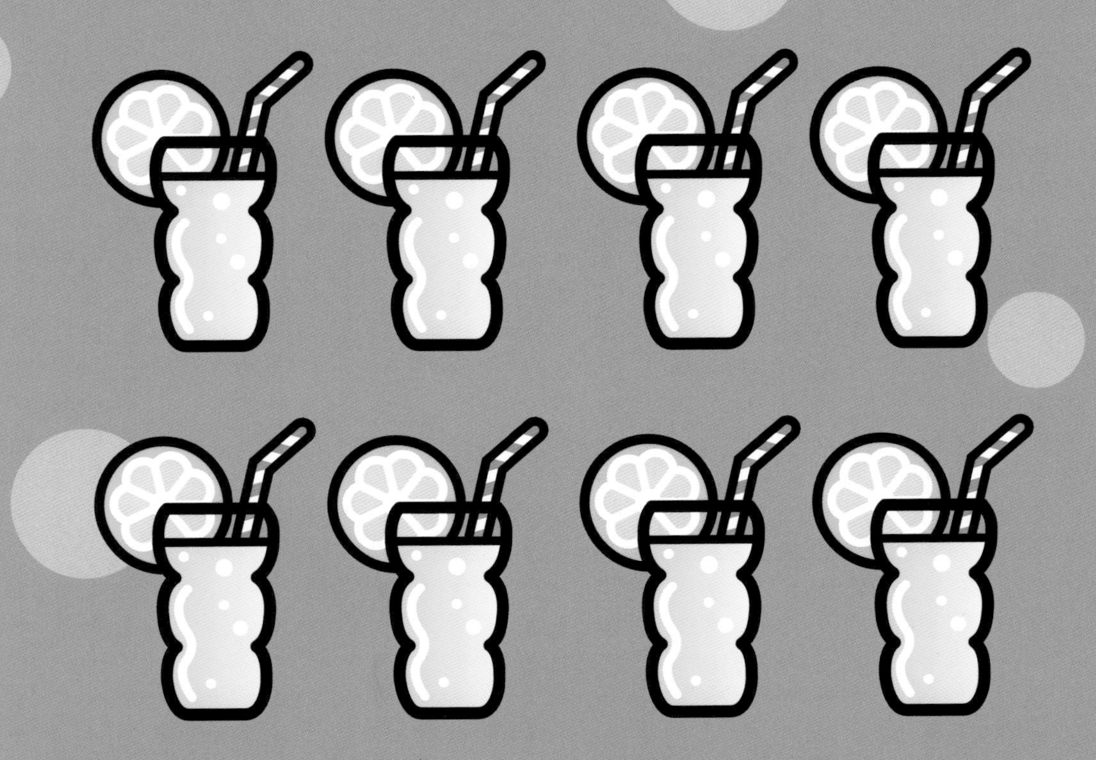

8

Eight glasses of lemonade are tangy and tart.

hello nine!

Nine friends together! And still more on the way.

hello ten!

10

Ten cookies are munchy, crunchy good.

hello eleven!

Eleven friends together!

hello twelve!

12

Twelve candies make the party extra sweet.

hello thirteen!

13

Thirteen friends together! Is everyone having fun?

hello fourteen!

14

Fourteen party horns add a cheery sound.

hello fifteen!

15

Fifteen friends and Mama and Papa, too!

hello sixteen!

16

Sixteen balloons make the party bright.

hello seventeen!

Seventeen friends and family! The more the merrier!

hello eighteen!

18

Eighteen party hats—now everyone is having fun.

hello nineteen!

19

Nineteen friends and family! The party is almost ready!

hello twenty!

20

Twenty presents! But who are they all for?

hello surprise!

Have you guessed already? This party is for you!

Can you count how many of each of these there are at the party?
ice creams
cookies
party horns
balloons
cupcakes
candies
presents
candy apples
lemonades
party hats

Answers for the party search!

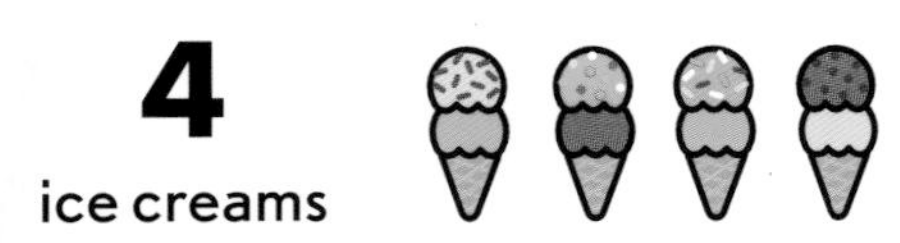

4 ice creams

10 cookies

14 party horns

16 balloons

2 cupcakes

12 candies

20 presents

6 candy apples

8 lemonades

18 party hats